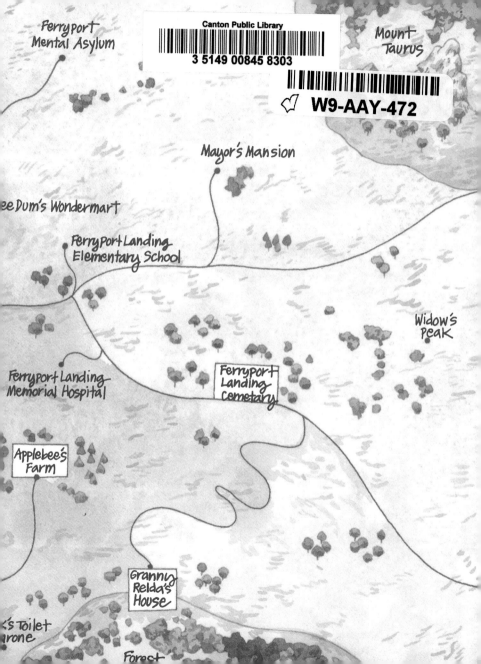

Ferryport
Mental Asylum

Mount
Taurus

Mayor's Mansion

ee Dum's Wondermart

Ferryport Landing
Elementary School

Widow's
Peak

Ferryport Landing
Memorial Hospital

Ferryport
Landing
Cemetery

Applebee's
Farm

Granny
Relda's
House

's Toilet
rone

Forest

A VERY GRIMM GUIDE

Blah, blah, blah.
I write books. Well, la-dee-dah!

Also by Michael Buckley:

IN THE SISTERS GRIMM SERIES:

IN THE NERDS SERIES:

A VERY GRIMM GUIDE

Inside The World of
The Sisters Grimm, Everafters,
Ferryport Landing, and
Everything in Between

By Michael Buckley

Amulet Books

New York

Based on *The Sisters Grimm* series, created by Michael Buckley

Library of Congress Cataloging-in-Publication Data has been applied
for and may be obtained from the Library of Congress.

ISBN-13: 978-1-4197-0201-3

Illustrations © Peter Ferguson except where otherwise noted below

Page 30: Illustration by Ivan Bilibin, *Beautiful Vasilisa*, 1900; Page 42: Etching by Ludwig Emil Grimm, courtesy of Brüder
Grimm-Gesellschaft, Kassel, Germany; Page 53: Photograph © Shuttershock/Jule Berlin; Page 60: Illustration by Arthur
Rackham, *A Midsummer's Night's Dream*, 1908; Page 64: Courtesy of Library of Congress Prints and Photographs Division
Washington, D.C.; Page 67: Illustration by Arthur Rackham, *Snowdrop and Other Tales by the Brothers Grimm*, 1920; Page
69: Illustration by Warwick Goble, *The Fairy Book*, 1913, courtesy of Brüder Grimm-Gesellschaft, Kassel, Germany; Page
72: Illustration by L. Leslie Brooke, *The Three Little Pigs*, 1904; Page 75: Engraving by T. Johnson after a painting by W.
B. Richmond, 1894; Page 82: Illustration by Edmund Dulac, *The Sleeping Beauty and Other Fairy Tales*, 1910; Page 87: Il-
lustration by D.J. Munro after drawings by Gustave Doré, *The Tales of Mother Goose*, 1901; Page 103: Illustration by William
Wallace Denslow, *The Wonderful Wizard of Oz*, 1900; Page 104: Illustration by William Wallace Denslow, *The Wonderful
Wizard of Oz*, 1900; Page 106: Photograph by Dana Hull, 1908; Page 110: Illustration by John Tenniel, *Alice's Adventures in
Wonderland*, 1865; Page 111: Illustration by Arthur Rackham, *Alice's Adventures in Wonderland*, 1907; Page 114: Illustration
by Arthur Rackham, *Hansel and Grethel and Other Tales by the Brothers Grimm*, 1920; Page 117: Illustration by John Tenniel,
Through the Looking-Glass, and What Alice Found There, 1871; Page 119: Illustration by Arthur Rackham, *Fairy Tales by Hans
Andersen*, 1932.

A Stonesong Press Book
Produced by The Stonesong Press, LLC
Designed by Ohioboy Art & Design

Printed and bound in China

10 9 8 7 6 5

ABRAMS The Art of Books
195 Broadway, New York, NY 10007
abramsbooks.com

To Raven "Rae" Katiasa Bliss—
an ultimate guide for an ultimate fan

I dedicate this book to ME
cause I truly amaze myself.

TABLE OF CONTENTS

PART ONE
FERRYPORT LANDING

PART TWO
THE GRIMMS

PART THREE
FRIENDS

PART FOUR
ENEMIES

ACKNOWLEDGMENTS

First and foremost, my gratitude goes to Joe Deasy, who knows this series better than anyone (including me). It was a no-brainer to ask him to help write this guide. Thanks for your hard work and friendship. Secondly, Alison Fargis and Ellen Scordato of the Stonesong Press who conceived, produced, and oversaw the design elements of every page. Thanks for your vision and passion. Alison, thanks for every day of our lives. Special thanks to Andy Taray of Ohioboy for his inspired designs and Alexis Seabrook for putting Ferryport Landing on the map (literally).

Thank you to Andrea Mayer of Brüder Grimm-Gesellschaft (Association of the Brothers Grimm) in Kassel, Germany for help with illustration research, and to Peter Ferguson for his deft hand and unlimited imagination.

A special note of thanks to my editors, Susan Van Metre and Maggie Lehrman, for seeing the potential in not only this series but in me. This guide is a dream come true. Thanks to everyone at Amulet Books and Abrams Books for all of their support and for continuing to invite me to the Christmas parties.

Thanks to Jacob and Wilhelm Grimm, Hans Christian Andersen, L. Frank Baum, Rudyard Kipling, Andrew Lang, Charles Perrault, Charles Dickens, Aesop, and everyone else who inspired this series.

But most of all—thank you, the fans and the readers who have gone down this rabbit hole with me since the first book. You have given me the ultimate job.

I'll thank you if you just shut up!

An Introduction by The
Trickster King

Hello minions! Nice to smell you! Welcome to A Very Grimm Guide—everything you ever wanted to know about me—your hero, Puck. That's right, me! Why not me? I'm awesome. Let's face it—no one reads these books because of Dog Face Sabrina and her sidekick Marshmallow. They read them to enjoy my delightful hijinks! Unfortunately, the loser who wrote this book thinks you might want to know about the other people that live in Ferryport Landing. HE IS WRONG and no matter what I said or threatened to leave on his pillow he would not listen.

So, basically, I was ready to wash my hands of the whole thing. After all, books and I are not friends. Reading has always made me barfy. That is until I found out how books are made. Did you know that an entire forest of trees was murdered to make this book? It's true! Then the corpses were mashed and smashed and then sliced into "paper." Yeah, the thing you're holding in your hands is a dead tree sliced like baloney! Well, that completely changed my attitude about books. In fact, I decided to learn to read just so I could spend more time with these creepy things.

And that's when I read this book and realized how painfully dull it is. The author wastes a lot of time on "insider information" about the Sisters Grimm books that he should be devoting to ME. There are so many exciting facts about me that you don't know; like my longest toenail (4 inches), my favorite foods (depends on if they are alive or dead), or what I like to wear to bed (footie pajamas made from Bigfoot skin).

So, I wrote all over the thing—I guess you could call them edits—to help explain why I, the Crown Prince of Faerie, Leader of Layabouts, Master of Morons, Nobleman of Knuckleheads, and Spiritual Leader of Juvenile Delinquents, am the true star of the Sisters Grimm books. So sit back and enjoy. Oh, and as a special treat I have rubbed my behind on every page at no extra charge (not available in the e-book edition—sorry, suckers!)

PART ONE

FERRYPORT LANDING

THE ORIGINS OF FERRYPORT LANDING

Contrary to popular belief, the stories told by the brothers Jacob and Wilhelm Grimm were not fairy tales but rather actual events the brothers witnessed as part of their careers as professional detectives. Characters such as Snow White, Sleeping Beauty, Little Red Riding Hood, and Prince Charming were not the creations of storytellers but actual people who occasionally got into a whole lot of trouble. Sometimes, that trouble was more than they could handle, and the Everafters (that's what fairy-tale characters like to be called) decided to move to America to seek a better life. Wilhelm Grimm decided to accompany them and help them settle in this new land. He hired a ship called the *Neuer Anfang* (New Beginning) and secured the deed for a large tract of land bordered by the Hudson River. This new town was called Fairyport Landing, and was originally intended as an exclusive Everafter territory, but soon humans moved in and tensions rose between the Everafters and their new neighbors. To protect the Everafters and keep the peace, Wilhelm turned to a powerful witch named Baba Yaga. Together the two cast a spell that confined the fairy-tale characters within the town's borders. But Baba Yaga made Wilhelm pay a price for his prison. If the Grimm family dies out or abandons the town, the Everafters will regain their freedom.

Unfortunately, the trouble did not end, and generations of Wilhelm's family have taken on the family business—keeping the peace, investigating any criminal Everafter activity, and documenting what they see.

 "We are Grimms and this is what we do."

GRIMM FAMILY TREE

WILHELM CARL GRIMM
(1786–1859) and his wife Henrietta had
Douglas Grimm in 1813.

THOMAS GRIMM
(1832–1836)

DOUGLAS GRIMM
(1813–went missing in 1860) and his wife
Delores had Spaulding (1830–1914), Thomas
(1832–1836), and Dessie Grimm (1835–1850).

DESSIE GRIMM
(1835–1850)

DOUGLAS GRIMM
(1847–1864)

SPAULDING GRIMM
(1830–1914) and his wife Jane Ella had Douglas (1847–1864) and Josef Grimm (1848–1927).

VESTA GRIMM
(1875–1960)

JOSEF GRIMM
(1848–1927) and his wife Anna had Vesta
(1875–1960), Trixie (1875–1963), and Peter
Grimm (1870–1947).

TRIXIE GRIMM
(1875–1963)

CHLOE GRIMM
(1915–1919)

PETER GRIMM
(1870–1947) and his wife Alison had Chloe
(1915–1919), Edwin (1925–1976), Matilda
(1928–1978), and Basil Grimm (1932–1994).

EDWIN GRIMM
(1925–1976)

MATILDA GRIMM
(1928–1978)

**JACOB ALEXANDER
GRIMM**
(1978)

BASIL GRIMM
(1932–1994) and his wife Relda had Henry
(1976) and Jacob Alexander Grimm (1978).

HENRY GRIMM
(1976) and his wife Veronica had Sabrina
(1998), Daphne (2002), and Basil Grimm
(2009).

SABRINA GRIMM
(1998)

BASIL GRIMM
(2009)

DAPHNE GRIMM
(2002)

1805
NEUER ANFANG (NEW BEGINNING) ARRIVES IN FAIRYPORT LANDING.

1825

After learning of a plot to invade and conquer the neighboring town of Cold Spring by a mysterious group of Everafters known as the Scarlet Hand, Wilhelm Grimm asks Baba Yaga to use her magic to erect a barrier around Fairyport Landing.

1859

Wilhelm Grimm dies. No Everafter attends his funeral, and his son Douglas sends his body back to Germany to be buried near his brother Jacob.

1860

Douglas Grimm mysteriously disappears. His body is never found.

DATE UNKNOWN
SNOW WHITE GIVES THE GRIMM FAMILY HER MAGIC MIRROR. IT CONTAINS THE HALL OF WONDERS AND IS GUARDED BY MIRROR.

1909

Spaulding Grimm gives the Black Knight the Vorpal blade to kill the Jabberwocky. Instead, the Knight cuts a hole through the barrier and escapes. Spaulding asks the Blue Fairy to break the blade into three pieces and scatter them.

1976

Henry Grimm is born.

1976

Edwin Grimm dies. Basil and Relda return with baby Henry to Ferryport Landing.

1978

Matilda Grimm dies of pneumonia

1978

Jacob Grimm is born

1993

AFTER DECADES OF FEAR, HAMSTEAD DEFEATS THE BIG BAD WOLF BY TURNING THE MONSTER'S HORN OF THE NORTH WIND AGAINST HIM. IN DOING SO, HAMSTEAD BRIEFLY BLOWS OUT THE WOLF SPIRIT, LEAVING A MYSTERIOUS MAN BEHIND. THE MAN KNOWS NOTHING OF HIS PAST. ESSENTIALLY, MR. CANIS IS "BORN."

1993

Relda takes Canis in despite protests from her sons and Basil.

1994

Henry and Jake briefly let down the barrier to allow Henry's girlfriend, Goldilocks, to leave Ferryport Landing. They unknowingly let down another magical barrier holding the deadly Jabberwocky, and it escapes.

1994

BASIL GRIMM DIES TRYING TO HELP JAKE FIGHT THE JABBER-WOCKY.

1994

Henry moves to New York City.

1994

Jake leaves Ferryport Landing and travels the world.

IMPORTANT EVENTS
IN GRIMM HISTORY

1910

HUMAN RESIDENTS VOTE TO HAVE THE TOWN'S NAME CHANGED FROM FAIRYPORT LANDING TO FERRYPORT LANDING.

1911

Trixie Grimm creates the Editor to prevent further changes to the Book of Everafter.

1944

Edwin and Matilda Grimm trick the giants into climbing the beanstalks and then cut them down, trapping them in the Cloud Kingdom.

DATE UNKNOWN

Matilda Grimm writes the pamphlet "Rumplestiltskin's Secret Nature."

**1974
BASIL AND RELDA ARE MARRIED AND TRAVEL THE WORLD ON A TWO-YEAR HONEYMOON.**

Where's "Puck Saves Our Lives Again"?

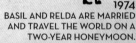

1995–1997

HENRY MEETS AND MARRIES VERONICA, THEN RETURNS TO FERRYPORT LANDING FOR ONE YEAR.

1997

Veronica becomes pregnant, and Henry, determined to keep his children out of the world that killed his father, leaves again for New York City.

1998

Sabrina is born.

2002

Daphne is born.

**2008
HENRY AND VERONICA DISAPPEAR. A RED HANDPRINT IS LEFT ON THE DASHBOARD— THE FIRST SIGN OF THE SCARLET HAND.**

2008

Sabrina and Daphne are put into the custody of the New York Department of Child Welfare and Ms. Smirt. For the next eighteen months, she places the girls with foster families, and each time, within days, the girls escape.

2009

Baby Basil Grimm is born.

**2009
SMIRT TAKES THE GIRLS TO LIVE WITH "THEIR GRANDMOTHER."**

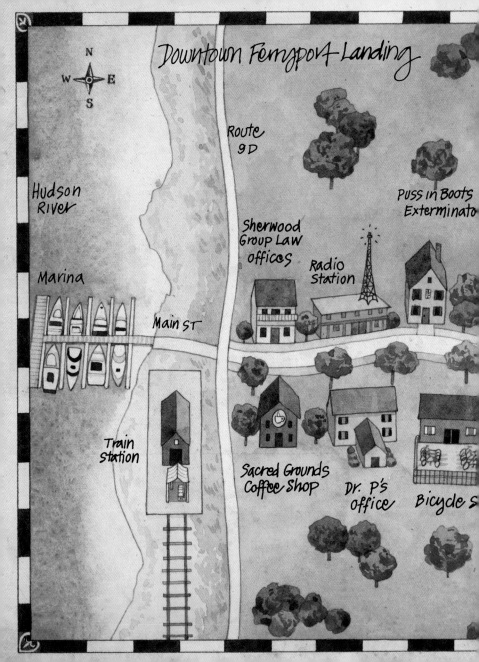

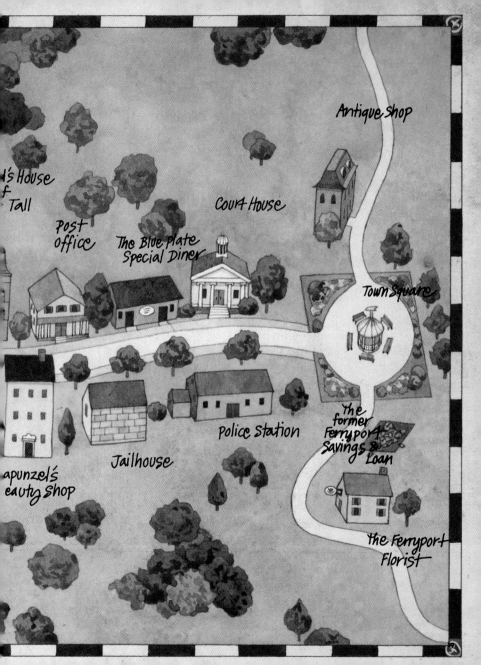

THE MANIFEST

OF THE

SHIP

NEUER ANFANG

Though many others would join the community in the years to come, including citizens of Oz, Kipling's jungles, Wonderland, and parts of America, these are the original founders of Fairyport Landing (aka Ferryport Landing).

NEUE

LIST OR MANIFEST OF ALIEN IMMIG

Required by the regulations of the Secretary of the Treasury of the United States, un
Commanding officer of any vessel having such

S.S.   NEUER ANFANG

1	2	3	4	5		6
NO. ON SHIP	NO. OF TICKETS	NAME IN FULL	HUMAN/BEAST/ FAIRYFOLK/ ODDITY	ENDOWED WITH FACULTY OF LANGUAGE?		CONDITION OF HEALTH?
				YES	NO	
01	1	Briar Rose	Human	Yes		good
02	"	Mallobarb	Fairy Folk	Yes		"
03	"	Buzzflower	Fairy Folk	Yes		"
04	"	Snow White	Human			"
05	7	The Seven Dwarfs	Human	Yes		"
06	1	The Wicked Queen	Human	Yes		"
07	"	Beauty	Human	Yes		"
08	"	The Beast	Beast	Yes		"
09	"	Jack The Giant Killer	Human	Yes		"
10	"	Rumpelstiltskin	Fairyfolk	Yes		"
11	"	Cinderella	Human	Yes		"
12	3	Cinderella's Mice	Beasties		No	"
13	2	Una & Elphbet (stepsisters)	Humans	Yes		"
14	1	Twildarose	Fairyfolk	Yes		"
15	1	Little Bo Peep	Human	Yes		"
16	12	Sheep	Beasties		No	"
17	1	Faithful John	Human	Yes		"
18	"	The Queen of Hearts	Human	Yes		"
19	50	Card Soldiers	Oddities	Yes		

FOR THE COMMISSIONER OF IMMIGRATION.

Congress approved ~~~~~~ to be delivered to the Commissioner of Immigration
n board upon arrival at a port in the United States.

rt of FAIRYPORT LANDING

1 NO. ON SHIP	2 NO. OF TICKETS	3 NAME IN FULL	4 HUMAN/BEAST/ FAIRYFOLK/ ODDITY	5 ENDOWED WITH FACULTY OR LANGUAGE?		6 CONDITION OF HEALTH?	
				YES	NO		
20	1	The White Rabbit	Beast	Yes		good	
21	"	The Mad Hatter	Human	Yes		Fair	
22	"	The Cheshire Cat	Beast		No	good	
23	2	Tweedledee and Tweedledum	Humans	Yes		"	
24	1	The Caterpillar	Beast	Yes		"	
25	"	Alice	Human	Yes		"	
26	"	Humpty Dumpty	Oddity	Yes		"	
27	3	Blind Mice	Beasts	Yes		"	
28	1	Gepetto	Human	Yes		"	
29	"	Ali Baba	Human	Yes		"	
30	40	Thieves	Humans	Yes		"	
31	1	Rapunzel	Human	Yes		"	
32	"	Chicken Little	Beast	Yes		Fair	
33	"	King Arthur	Human	Yes		good	
34	"	Lancelot	Human	Yes		"	
35	"	Sir Foot	Human	Yes		"	
36	n/a	Various Knights of the Round Table	Human	Yes		"	
37	1	Guinevere	Human	Yes		"	
38	"	Morgan le Fay	Human	Yes		"	

AFFIDAVIT OF SURGEON.

LIST OR MANIFEST OF ALIEN IMMIGR

Required by the regulations of the Secretary of the Treasury of the United States, und
Commanding officer of any vessel having such p

S.S.   NEUER ANFANG   A

NO. ON SHIP	NO. OF TICKETS	NAME IN FULL	HUMAN/BEAST/ FAIRYFOLK/ ODDITY	ENDOWED WITH FACULTY OF LANGUAGE?		CONDITION OF HEALTH?
				YES	NO	
39	1	Mordred	Human	Yes		Poor
40	"	Baba Yaga	Human	Yes		Good
41	"	Walking Chicken Hut	Oddity		No	"
42	"	Bright Morning	Oddity	Yes		"
43	"	Dark Night	Oddity	Yes		"
44	"	Red Sun	Oddity	Yes		"
45	"	Frau Pfefferkuchenhaus	Human	Yes		"
46	"	Hansel	Human	yes		"
47	"	Gretel	Human	Yes		"
48	"	Ice Queen	Fairyfolk	Yes		"
49	"	Little Miss Muffet	Human	Yes		"
50	"	Spider	Beast		No	"
51	"	The Frog Prince	Oddity	Yes		"
52	"	Princess	Human	Yes		"
53	"	Winter, Queen of the Crows	Beast	Yes		"
54	"	The Nightingale	Beast		No	"
55	"	The Old Woman who live in a Shoe	Human	Yes		"
56	N/A	Children (too many to count)	Humans	Yes		"
57	1	Little Red Riding Hood	Human	Yes		Good

AFFIDAVIT OF THE MASTER OR COMMANDING OFFICER, OR FIRST OR SECOND OFFICER

FOR THE COMMISSIONER OF IMMIGRATION.

Congress approved ~~~~~~~, to be delivered to the Commissioner of Immigration
a board upon arrival at a port in the United States.

t of FAIRYPORT LANDING

1 NO. ON SHIP	2 NO. OF TICKETS.	3 NAME IN FULL	4 HUMAN/BEAST/ FAIRYFOLK/ ODDITY	5 ENDOWED WITH FACULTY OF LANGUAGE? YES	NO	6 CONDITION OF HEALTH?	
58	1	The Big Bad Wolf	Beast	Yes		good	
89	1	Goldilocks	Human	Yes		"	
60	3	Bears	Beasties		No	"	
61	1	Howard Hatchett	Human	Yes		"	
62	10	Dragons	Oddities		No	"	
63	1	Iron John	Human	Yes		"	
64	3	Little Pigs	Beasties	Yes		"	
65	1	Grendel	Oddity		No	"	
66	10	Frost Giants	Fairyfolk	Yes		"	
67	1	Oberon	Fairyfolk	Yes		"	
68	"	Titania	Fairyfolk	Yes		"	
69	"	Puck	Fairyfolk	Yes		"	
70	"	Mustardseed	Fairyfolk	Yes		"	
71	"	Mothe	Fairyfolk	Yes		"	
72	"	Cobweb	Fairyfolk	Yes		"	
73	N/A	Pixies (too many to count)	Fairyfolk		No	"	
74	1	The Blue Fairy	Fairyfolk	Yes		"	
75	"	Mother Goose	Oddity	Yes		"	
76	1	The Emperor (listed as	Human	Yes		Fair	

MENT OF SURGEON.

NEUE

LIST OR MANIFEST OF ALIEN IMMIG

Required by the regulations of the Secretary of the Treasury of the United States, un
Commanding officer of any vessel having such

S.S. NEUER ANFANG

1	2	3	4	5		6	
NO. ON SHIP	NO. OF TICKETS	NAME IN FULL	HUMAN/BEAST/ FAIRYFOLK/ ODDITY	ENDOWED WITH FACULTY OF LANGUAGE?		CONDITION OF HEALTH?	
				YES	NO		
77	1	The Black Knight	Human	Yes		Good	
78	"	Robin Hood	Human	Yes		"	
79	"	Will Scarlet	Human	Yes		"	
80	"	Friar Tuck	Human	Yes		"	
81	"	Little John	Human	Yes		"	
82	20	Merry Man	Humans	Yes		"	
83	1	Maid Marian	Human	Yes		"	
84	"	Sheriff Notingham	Human	Yes		"	
85	"	BlueBear	Human	Yes		"	
86	"	The Cow that jumps over the moon	Beast	Yes		"	
87	"	Little Boy Blue	Human	Yes		"	
88	"	Hans the Hedgehog	Oddity	Yes		"	
89	"	Puss in Boots	Beast	Yes		"	
90	"	Old King Cole	Human	Yes		"	
91	"	Rip Van Winkle	Human	Yes		Fair	
92	"	The Butcher	Human	Yes		good	
93	"	The Baker	Human	Yes		Fair	
94	"	The Candlestick Maker	Human	Yes		Poor	
95	"	The Pied Piper	Human	Yes		Good	

NFANG

FOR THE COMMISSIONER OF IMMIGRATION.

Congress approved _____ to be delivered to the Commissioner of Immigration
board upon arrival at a port in the United States.

of *FAIRYPORT LANDING*

1	2	3	4	5		6		
NO. ON SHIP	NO. OF TICKETS	NAME IN FULL	HUMAN/BEAST/ FAIRYFOLK/ ODDITY	ENDOWED WITH FACULTY OR LANGUAGE?		CONDITION OF HEALTH?		
				YES	NO			
96	1	Sinbad	Human	Yes		Good		
97	15	Sailors	Humans	Yes		"		
98	1	The Ugly Duckling	Beast	Yes		"		
99	1	The Gingerbread man	Oddity	Yes		"		
100	7	Grim Brothers	Beasts	Yes		"		
101	1,443	Lilliputians	Oddities	Yes		"		
102	1	Gulliver	Human	Yes		"		
103	12	Houyhnhnms	Oddities	Yes		"		
104	16	Jabberwockies	Oddities	Limited		"		
105	33	Yahoos	Oddities	Yes		"		
106	27	Leprechauns	Fairyfolk	Yes		"		
107	9	Ogres	Fairyfolk	Some		"		
108	84	Trolls	Fairyfolk	Yes		"		
109	13	Cyclopes	Oddities		No	"		
110	423	Gnomes	Fairyfolk	Yes		"		
111	144	Elves	Fairyfolk	Yes		"		
112	28	Goblins	Fairyfolk	Some		"		
113	56	Hobgoblins	Fairyfolk	Some		"		
114	25	Magic Mirrors	Oddities	Yes		"		

PART TWO

THE GRIMMS

I keep a record of every booger I pick

⇜ FROM THE GRIMM COLLECTION ⇝

FAIRY-TALE ACCOUNTS

| YEAR | 1829 | NAME | Wilhelm Grimm |

(Translated from the original German)

While I should have noticed this before the attempted attack on Cold Spring, I fear that the claustrophobia afflicting many Everafters is spreading out of control. I have recruited the Blue Fairy and Baba Yaga to help in expanding the space within our borders. They plan to add hundreds of square miles of forests and mountains, all contained within the original border of the town. They have assured me that this will not weaken the barrier and will ease the restlessness so many Everafters are exhibiting.

FAIRY-TALE ACCOUNTS

YEAR	1859	NAME	Douglas Grimm

Father died on Wednesday. Today I held a memorial service for him near the site where the courthouse will soon be built. No one attended. Not a single one of these Everafters, as they now call themselves, bothered to show up and pay their respects. After all Wilhelm Grimm did for them.

I've arranged for his body to be sent back to Germany. Mother is going as well. She's had enough of this new world.

magical object!
CINDERELLA'S FAIRY GODMOTHER'S WAND

The Changing Wand once belonged to Cinderella's fairy godmother, Twilarose. Like most fairy-godmother wands, it has a star on the end. When you wave it three times, you can give someone a makeover. Sabrina and Daphne soon discovered that it could also completely change the appearance of someone, and they used it to disguise themselves as Momma Bear and the Tin Woodsman in order to sneak into Mayor Charming's fundraising ball. The Changing Wand has a built-in timer, and at a predetermined time, the magic spell expires.

SABRINA

Sabrina Grimm was an ordinary girl living in New York City with her mom, dad, and sister, Daphne, until one night her parents went missing. Sabrina had to grow up fast to take care of her little sister as they bounced from one foster family to the next. Many of their so-called caregivers were either criminally insane or insanely criminal. All the chaos made Sabrina tough, clever, brave, and extremely tenacious—which came in handy in the sisters' ingenious escapes from foster homes and unyielding defiance of their caseworker, Ms. Smirt.

Barf face

"If you haven't noticed I don't have any magical powers. I'm not an Everafter. I'm just a girl from New York City."

Boring

Hi-larious!

Sabrina feared that their parents abandoned them, and it made her suspicious, impulsive, sneaky, and stubborn, too. When the girls were taken in by their long-presumed-dead grandmother Relda Grimm, those traits kicked into high gear, making life very hard for the sisters.

Sabrina was determined to get Daphne away from Ferryport Landing, even if she had to drag her, but the truth about the town and the Grimm family tree could not be hidden forever. Granny was kidnapped by a giant, and the girls mounted a daring rescue. Since then, Sabrina has come face to face with Rumplestiltskin, the Jabberwocky, the Blue Fairy, the Wizard of Oz, Cinderella, and a seriously delusional Little Red Riding Hood, among many others.

With help from Granny Relda, Mr. Canis, and the frustratingly annoying Puck, she began her training as a fairy-tale detective following in the footsteps of generations of Grimms before her. But what truly matters to Sabrina is keeping her family together—no matter what the Grimms' main nemesis, the Master, and his band of evil Everafters, the Scarlet Hand, throw her way.

That's it?! You could write a book on her stink!

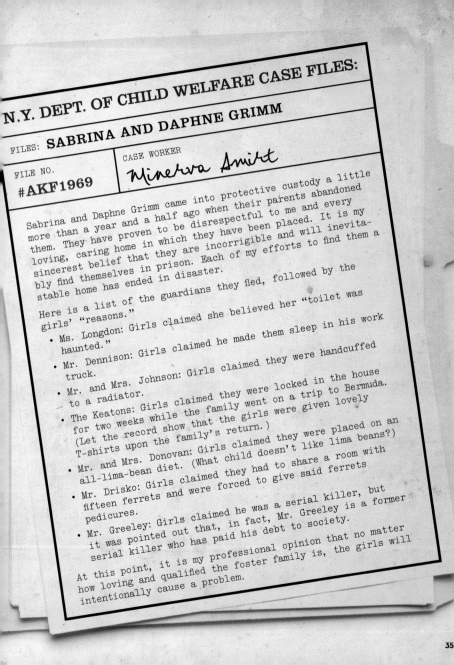

N.Y. DEPT. OF CHILD WELFARE CASE FILES:

FILES: **SABRINA AND DAPHNE GRIMM**

FILE NO.	CASE WORKER
#AKF1969	*Minerva Smirt*

Sabrina and Daphne Grimm came into protective custody a little more than a year and a half ago when their parents abandoned them. They have proven to be disrespectful to me and every loving, caring home in which they have been placed. It is my sincerest belief that they are incorrigible and will inevitably find themselves in prison. Each of my efforts to find them a stable home has ended in disaster.

Here is a list of the guardians they fled, followed by the girls' "reasons."

- Ms. Longdon: Girls claimed she believed her "toilet was haunted."
- Mr. Dennison: Girls claimed he made them sleep in his work truck.
- Mr. and Mrs. Johnson: Girls claimed they were handcuffed to a radiator.
- The Keatons: Girls claimed they were locked in the house for two weeks while the family went on a trip to Bermuda. (Let the record show that the girls were given lovely T-shirts upon the family's return.)
- Mr. and Mrs. Donovan: Girls claimed they were placed on an all-lima-bean diet. (What child doesn't like lima beans?)
- Mr. Drisko: Girls claimed they had to share a room with fifteen ferrets and were forced to give said ferrets pedicures.
- Mr. Greeley: Girls claimed he was a serial killer, but it was pointed out that, in fact, Mr. Greeley is a former serial killer who has paid his debt to society.

At this point, it is my professional opinion that no matter how loving and qualified the foster family is, the girls will intentionally cause a problem.

MARSHMALLOW

DAPHNE

Unlike her sister, Daphne is a hilarious ball of optimism, completely enchanted with their new lives as fairy-tale detectives. Living in Ferryport Landing is like living inside a bedtime story, where all her favorite characters have come to life. Not only did Granny Relda offer the girls a real family, they got to be detectives who solve crimes committed by characters from storybooks! She's formed deep bonds with Relda, Canis, Puck, and Elvis. Unlike Sabrina, who has an unhealthy relationship with magic, Daphne is incredibly comfortable with wands and magic shoes—delighting in the amazing things they can do. Despite her growing independence, Daphne still turns to Sabrina in times of need.

"You are so punk rock!"

FUTURE SABRINA AND DAPHNE

When Sabrina and Daphne are pulled into a hole in time, they find themselves fifteen years in the future. The Ferryport Landing they step into is filled with dragons that hunt humans, monsters running amok, and the Master in total control of the world. When the girls are attacked by a crazed Big Bad Wolf, they are rescued by their future selves. Future Sabrina is a war-tested fighter armed with daggers, a sword, and even a whip. Future Daphne is a magic-wielding sorceress with a jagged scar across her face and a lifetime of bitterness. Still, the most shocking thing about the future for the girls is not how they turn out but rather the man Sabrina grows up to marry—a certain winged boy who has become a dashing winged husband. When the girls return to their own time, they make a pact to change as much as they can about the future, and when they next meet their future selves, Daphne's heart is not so cold, and her scar is nowhere to be found.

—— magical object! ——
THE SHOES OF SWIFTNESS

As you might guess from the name, they allow the wearer to run at incredible speeds. Sabrina used them to escape the Cruel Crustacean, rocketing out of the water and running on top of it (while dragging Daphne and Jake). They once belonged to Jack the Giant Killer but were acquired by the Grimm family at some point in time. They are stored in the Hall of Wonders in a room set aside for magical footwear.

Scared as usual! Losers.

RELDA GRIMM
AKA GRANNY RELDA

At first glance, Relda Grimm seems gentle, compassionate, and patient, but she's also quite resourceful, determined, and incredibly smart (and don't forget the broadsword and a battle-ax she keeps by her bed). She never goes out without her trademark hat with an appliqué of a big, fuzzy sunflower in the middle, her handbag, and her trusty friend, Elvis. Relda is at her most dangerous behind the wheel of a car; however, Sabrina would argue that Relda's cooking is as just as dangerous as her driving. What she may lack in driving and culinary skills, she more than makes up for as a detective. Trained by her late husband, Basil, Relda has taken over the family responsibility despite the fact that she married into it. Now, her job is preparing her granddaughters for the day they will take over the family business.

> "Hatred can grow, child, into something terrible and beyond your control."

Hey, old lady! I'm hungry!

FEARSOME FOLKTALES

IN THE GRIMMS' "THE GOOSE MAID," A SERVING MAID WHO PASSES HERSELF OFF AS A PRINCESS IS PUNISHED BY BEING PLACED NAKED IN A NAIL-STUDDED BARREL THAT IS HARNESSED TO TWO HORSES WHO DRAG IT THROUGH TOWN UNTIL SHE IS DEAD.

JACOB AND WILHELM GRIMM

AKA "THE BROTHERS GRIMM"
JACOB (1785–1863), WILHELM (1786–1859)

Inspired by the stories they heard during their childhood in Germany, Jacob and Wilhelm Grimm began researching, collecting, and transcribing folk tales in the early nineteenth century. Many of these stories were violent, filled with terrifying villains and horrible deaths. Naturally, kids loved them. This surprised the Brothers Grimm, who had written the books for scholars and adults. The first edition was full of academic footnotes and wasn't illustrated. Wilhelm went through and rewrote many of the stories, replacing evil mothers with wicked stepmothers, for example, and removing any mention of things he considered inappropriate for children. In 1812, they published the first edition of *Kinder-und Hausmärchen* (*Children's and Household Tales*), which consisted of eighty-six stories. Over the years, they added to their collections, removed some stories, and revised some others. When the seventh and final edition of the work was published in 1857, it contained 211 stories, including versions of many of the most famous tales: "Cinderella," "Sleeping Beauty," "Little Red Riding Hood," "Rumplestiltskin," "Snow White," and "Rapunzel." It's since been translated into 160 languages, and it's arguably the most famous and influential work of literature in the German language.

Relda's Squid Ink Spaghetti with Curry Sauce and Chartreuse Meatballs

FOR THE MEATBALLS:

1/2 pound ground pork

1/2 pound ground veal

1/2 pound ground shamrock higginbottoms

1 cup panko breadcrumbs

1 cup Parmesan cheese

1/2 white onion, chopped

2 teaspoons salt

1 egg, beaten

olive oil

Combine the meats, higginbottoms, bread crumbs, Parmesan, onion, egg, and 1 cup warm water in a bowl. Using hands, combine mixture, and then roll into 2-inch balls.

Heat the olive oil in a large skillet. Place the meatballs in the pan, and cook over medium heat until brown. Careful! The higginbottoms will spark when they hit the pan!

FOR THE SAUCE:

olive oil

1 1/2 large white onions, chopped

3 cloves garlic, minced

1 pinch of Pegasus hair

28 ounces canned, whole, peeled tomatoes

1 stick of butter

2 tablespoons cumin

2 tablespoons curry paste

1 teaspoon of Dragon Fire

1 pair of protective goggles

Making the sauce—Heat the olive oil in the same skillet. Saute onions over medium heat, about 10 minutes. Add garlic and Pegasus hair, turn heat to high, and cook for 5 minutes. Open the windows at this point as the Pegasus hair can smoke and smell like feet. Add the tomatoes, butter, cumin, and paste, and heat through for 5 more minutes. Stir in the Dragon Fire, and immediately put on the protective goggles. Once the sauce explodes four times, add the meatballs to the sauce, cover, and simmer for 30 minutes.

FOR SERVING: 1 1/2 pounds fresh squid-ink spaghetti, cooked according to Little Mermaid's instructions / Freshly grated Parmesan

OBITUARIES

LIFELONG FERRYPORT LANDING RESIDENT BASIL GRIMM, DEAD AT 62

FERRYPORT LANDING

Lifelong Ferryport Landing resident Basil Grimm, sixty-two, was killed last night in the forests near Mount Taurus. A family spokesperson, Mr. Canis, claims his death was caused by an animal attack that the sheriff's office has declared a tragic accident. Police have quarantined the area and warn ALL residents to avoid the woods until the creature is found and captured.

Mr. Grimm, a descendent of the town's founder, Wilhelm Grimm, was a well-known amateur sleuth who was often at the center of solving some of the town's biggest crimes. Mr. Grimm was also deeply involved in local politics and city planning, and his name was often mentioned as a possible candidate for mayor, though his wife claims he was never interested in the office.

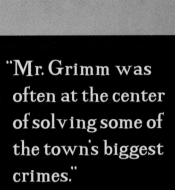

"Mr. Grimm was often at the center of solving some of the town's biggest crimes."

He was married for thirty-two years, having met his wife, Relda, in Berlin where the two enjoyed a whirlwind romance. Just one week later, they married and embarked on a two-year honeymoon traveling the world—including Istanbul, the Yukon, Hawaii, the Amazon, South Africa, and the Himalayas, just to name a few. Shortly after the birth of their first son, Henry, they returned to Ferryport Landing where they lived until his death.

Basil is survived by his wife, Relda, and their two sons, Henry and Jacob.

JACOB ALEXANDER GRIMM

AKA JAKE, UNCLE JAKE

Unlike his mild-mannered older brother, Jake Grimm is a bit of an adventurer who finds himself in trouble more often than not. (He's got the broken nose to prove it!) Jake is a master of magic, and in his travels he's collected powerful items of enchantment, many of which he keeps in the many pockets of his trench coat. Despite his charm and ever-present smile, Jake carries a lot of guilt and pain in his heart. He blames himself for the death of his father and for driving his brother away. Sadly, when he finally opens his heart once more to the lovely Briar Rose, her life is cut short by a dragon controlled by the Scarlet Hand.

THE ITEMS IN JAKE'S COAT

Satin Surgeon's Salve

An Invulnerability Stone

The Amulet of Roona

Evil Eye Drops

Curse B Gone

Witch Hazel Repellent

The Eye of Omega
(one of the Phantom Stones)

Pixie dust

A back-up pair of Invisible Underwear
(from the Emperor himself)

FAIRY-TALE ACCOUNTS

YEAR	1909	NAME	Spaulding Grimm

The Everafters grow ever more agitated as they feel they are being unjustly punished for the behavior of a bad few. They have a point. A majority of our citizens are good, hard working folk. Yet, there are those that have truly dark hearts and intentions.

Take the case of the Black Knight. Even after betraying me and escaping the town, he chose to leave the Vorpal blade behind. I can only assume he did so because he knows there is no other way to kill the Jabberwocky. Without it, Fairyport Landing couldn't defend itself. Regardless, it served his purposes. Also noteworthy, he didn't choose to take anyone with him. He could have freed the town. For this, I feel a sense of respect, even gratitude, toward him. In fact, I wouldn't have known the sword could slice the barrier had he not done it. Who knows what could have happened had Rumplestiltskin or the Wolf discovered this? I will have to find a way to hide this sword. Perhaps breaking it into pieces will prevent it falling into the wrong hands. If only we had some sort of place to store such magical items.

So today the Knight has me wondering. Are there any amongst us that are truly good and truly evil? Wilhelm believed that even the basest villain could change. Until I see it happen, I feel it's best to leave the barrier around the town.

HENRY AND VERONICA GRIMM

Henry grew up fully embracing the Grimm family legacy. He and his brother, Jake, were wild boys growing up in Ferryport Landing as they trained to be fairy-tale detectives. Henry even fell in love with a grown-up Goldilocks. When a well-meaning Jake found a way to drop the magical barrier, he unwittingly freed a nightmarish monster known as the Jabberwocky from a magic spell. The beast killed Henry and Jake's father, and in despair, Henry left town. Once he was in New York City, he began to rebuild his life and met the lovely Veronica.

Feisty, independent, and beautiful, it's easy to see why Veronica is Henry's true love. After they married, the couple moved back to Ferryport Landing briefly, and

Love is barfy.

48

Veronica began to learn the ropes of the family business. But when she and Henry learned there was a baby on the way, the couple decided it was best to leave the dangers of the town behind. Henry swore he'd never return and vowed that his children would have nothing to do with magic, Everafters, or Ferryport Landing. Henry even went so far as to tell the girls that their grandmother Relda had died before they were born and forbade them from reading fairy tales. Veronica, however, didn't share his views and worked with New York City's small Everafter community in secret. She helped the struggling community find work, build schools, and adapt to modern American life. She even developed a close friendship with the Wizard of Oz, who sadly turned out to be a member of the Scarlet Hand. He kidnapped Henry and Veronica and handed them over to the Master, who cursed them with a sleeping spell that can only be broken by true love's kiss.

FEARSOME FOLKTALES

IN THE GRIMMS' VERSION OF "THE FROG PRINCE," THE FROG IS TURNED INTO A PRINCE, NOT BY A KISS, BUT WHEN THE PRINCESS HURLS THE FROG AGAINST A WALL.

ELVIS

Named after the King of Rock and Roll, Elvis Presley, this big dog is a 200-pound Great Dane. Relda calls her overly-affectionate sidekick "her boyfriend" and says he has the best sniffing nose in the county. He's an essential tool in Granny's detective work and often acts as the family's protector, especially when a monster rears its ugly head. Still, you have to keep an eye on him. He has a knack for stealing sausages from the fridge, which make him terribly gassy! When the girls visit the future, they meet his grandchildren—four rowdy pups named after other rock and roll royalty: John, Paul, George, and Ringo.

FART!

BABY BASIL

Two-year-old Basil's short life has been marred by shocking events. Stolen from Veronica while she lay under the effects of a sleeping spell, the boy was raised by the Master to be a vessel for his own dark soul. None of the other Grimms knew he existed until he was almost a toddler.

magical object!
ALADDIN'S FLYING CARPET

One of the most famous and useful magical items in the world, Aladdin's fabled flying carpet can act as a person's personal taxicab. All the rider must do is announce a destination and the carpet will take them there—even if the rider does not have directions.

HANS CHRISTIAN ANDERSEN

Hans Christian Andersen was a Danish writer who became internationally famous for his children's stories (many of which were written for adults). Some, like "The Emperor's New Clothes," were based on folk tales, but others, such as "The Steadfast Tin Soldier," he created entirely himself. "The Ugly Duckling," "The Little Mermaid," and "The Little Match Girl" are three of his most famous original tales. In fact, "The Little Mermaid" was first written as a ballet. Andersen may have wanted to be a dancer; he loved singing and acting, but he was tall and awkward with a very large nose. The other children teased him about his appearance. Thus, "The Ugly Duckling" may have been the story closest to his heart. He once remarked that the tale was "a reflection of my own life" and often referred to it as his autobiography. His stories contain strong moral lessons and don't always have happy endings. Nevertheless, children and adults across the world loved them, and still do. The Danish are proud of Andersen, and they have a statue of the Little Mermaid in Copenhagen's harbor. International Children's Book Day is celebrated on his birthday, April 2. There's even a statue of him in New York's Central Park, which acts as the magical entrance to the Kingdom of Faerie in the *Sisters Grimm* books.

That's hilarious!

𝄢 FEARSOME FOLKTALES

IN ANDERSEN'S "THE LITTLE MERMAID," THE PRINCE MARRIES ANOTHER WOMAN. SEEKING REVENGE, THE LITTLE MERMAID SNEAKS INTO HIS BEDROOM TO MURDER HIM BUT AT THE LAST MOMENT CHANGES HER MIND. SHE THEN THROWS HERSELF OFF A CLIFF.

FAIRY-TALE ACCOUNTS

YEAR 1910 **NAME** *Trixie Grimm*

The Book of Everafter is exhilarating. Reginald complains that I am away inside its pages for too long, but he can't know what it's like to visit so many places I have only heard of in our family's histories. (He's been a grouch, as I still refuse to take his name.) Unfortunately, there are some rather bizarre side effects that I did not intend. For one, the stories are all too fragile, and secondly any little change seems to affect the real world when I step back into it. I'm working on a solution. Like the magic mirror, I believe this book needs a guardian—someone who can put things right when the stories fall apart.

---

magical object!
THE TRAVELER'S CHEST

Jake borrowed it from the Andersen triplets—the last living descendents of Hans Christian Andersen. The chest appears to be a large, empty box. The user announces a place they would like to visit then opens the lid to find a staircase leading down. At the bottom is a door that opens into the traveler's destination.

PART THREE

FRIENDS

"I concentrate on all the people
I hurt when I was unable
to control myself... It helps
remind me of my guilt."

MR. CANIS

AKA THE BIG BAD WOLF, THE (REAL) WOODCUTTER, TOBIAS CLAY

On first impression, Mr. Canis appears to be quite old, skinny, and frail. But looks can be deceiving. This withered old man hides a monster inside of him named the Big Bad Wolf. It's not easy keeping the beast at bay, but with the right amount of meditation, determination, and yoga, he has learned to tap into the monster's incredible abilities without releasing its rage. He has shown a super strength and a keen sense of smell, which come in handy for Relda, who has been his companion and protector for almost fifteen years. Before that, he was an unstoppable killing machine, but it was his own destructive power that made him a man. The horn of the North Wind, which provided his "huff and puff," was used against him by Sheriff Hamstead—taming the monster and allowing the "Canis" personality to emerge. Mr. Canis didn't know who he was or how he'd gotten there, but he had vague memories of what the Wolf had done and the guilt he now feels is unbearable.

---
magical object!
THE HORN OF THE NORTH WIND

It may look like a silly children's toy, but it's one of the most powerful weapons in Ferryport Landing. In fact, it's the "secret weapon" the three pigs used to defeat the Big Bad Wolf. The user faces in the direction of his or her target then blows into the kazoo, creating a massive wall of wind as powerful as a hurricane. Capable of blowing a house away, it also was used to temporarily blow the murderous spirit out of Canis.

PUCK

AKA THE TRICKSTER KING; PRINCE OF FAERIE; EMPEROR OF PIXIES, BROWNIES; HOBGOBLINS; ELVES; AND GNOMES; ROBIN GOODFELLOW; THE IMP; MASTER OF MAYHEM; SAVIOR OF THE SHIFTLESS; ETC. . . . ETC.

While Puck claims he's a "supreme villain" and world famous scoundrel, he oddly enough spends a lot of time playing the hero. Puck has been around for 4,000 years and has been great story material for writers like William Shakespeare and Rudyard Kipling, and he would be the first to tell you so. As the son of King Oberon and Queen Titania, Puck is a fairy with the ability to fly. But don't mistake him for Peter Pan, or he'll use his flute to summon his loyal swarm of pixies to poke you like a million bees. He despises that tight-wearing nitwit. Unlike Peter Pan, Puck can also transform into a variety of different animals—sometimes to lend a helping hand but more often than not to pull a prank on Sabrina. Though he's incredibly immature and smells like a compost pile, Sabrina finds herself drawn to him. Much to his chagrin, he kind of likes her, too.

This isn't me!!

THIS is the picture you chose?! Gross!

I should have kissed the monkey!

"I see everything that goes on around here."

MIRROR

Mirror is the guardian of the magic mirror from the story of Snow White. He was the first enchanted mirror created by the Wicked Queen and serves as the template for all those that came after. His main job is to serve his master as an all-seeing eye and as the guardian of the Hall of Wonders, which exists inside the mirror's reflection. On the outside, he appears as a floating, bald head, but when you step into his home, he's really a short, chubby man in a black suit and tie who enjoys tanning, Pilates, facials, and studying his own reflection. Sabrina often confides in Mirror, feeling he's the only one she can talk to. And, he's always there for her because Mirror can't leave the confines of the Hall of Wonders.

─── **magical object!** ───
THE WICKED WITCH'S GOLDEN CAP

Seen in Baum's *Wonderful Wizard of Oz*, it's a cap used by the Wicked Witch that grants her the ability to summon a race of flying monkeys. It's held in the Hall of Wonders in the room labeled "Magical Hats," but it might be hard to find due to its unusual appearance. It's a gold-colored hard hat with a can of soda strapped to each side. Tubes run out of the cans and dangle below the chin strap. On the front of the cap are the words "Emerald City Green Sox." According to Mirror, the Wicked Witch was a huge baseball fan. To use the cap one must stand on their right leg and say "Ep-pe, pep-pe, kak-ke. Hil-lo, hol-lo, hel-lo, ziz-zy, zuz-zy, zik."

His face gave me 7 years of bad luck! Har-har!

PRINCE WILLIAM CHARMING

AKA MAYOR CHARMING, BILLY

The name Prince Charming evokes images of heroic deeds, chivalry, and a handsome man with a good heart. Sadly, times have changed. Charming is no longer a prince of a man—in fact, he can come off as selfish, petty, arrogant, and callous. But don't judge him too harshly—most of his motivations center on winning the heart of his former love, Snow White, who left him at the altar and ruined their happily ever after. Since then, he's married Briar Rose, Cinderella, and Rapunzel, but his heart has always been Snow's. Regardless of how he comes off, when it comes to the big decisions, Charming will eventually make the noble choice.

FEARSOME FOLKTALES

THERE ARE THOUSANDS OF VARIATIONS OF THE CINDERELLA STORY GOING BACK AS FAR AS 2,200 YEARS AGO TO THE ANCIENT GREEKS AND EGYPTIANS.

Love it! ↓

AT THE END OF THE GRIMM'S "CINDERELLA," THE WICKED STEPSISTERS HAVE THEIR EYES PECKED OUT BY CINDERELLA'S PIGEON FRIENDS AS PUNISHMENT FOR THEIR MISTREATMENT OF THE GIRL.

"Remember, vote early and vote often."

CHARMING MUSEUM OPENS

Today Mayor William Charming opened the William Charming Memorial Museum for Memorials of William Charming, which will house the many memorial works commissioned by the mayor of himself. Included are sculptures, fountains, paintings, tapestries, Etch A Sketch, hedgerows, finger paintings, as well several biographical films starring Charming himself.

Fun for all ages, but absolutely no children will be allowed entry.

MAYORAL UPSET

In a stunning upset, incumbent Mayor William Charming was defeated by dark horse candidate Mrs. Q. O. Heart. Upon hearing news of his loss Charming remarked, "My museum is on fire!" noting the hundreds of enthusiastic Heart supporters spraying gasoline onto the blaze. Thankfully, the fire was quickly extinguished when an enormous boulder fell from the sky, seemingly from nowhere, crushing the museum to dust and elating the crowd. Charming was unavailable for further comment.

CHARMING STILL MISSING

Former Mayor William Charming is still missing three weeks after his defeat at the polls. Mayor Heart reiterated her pledge to send out a search party as soon as Charming is found.

Enough with the love stuff!

"I won't marry someone who wants to take care of me. I'm going to take care of myself."

SNOW WHITE

Snow has grown up considerably since her story began hundreds of years ago. Back when she lived on her family's lands, she coasted on her looks and didn't worry much about her brain: "In a nutshell, I was dumb." But what really bothered her was the realization that she couldn't take care of herself. So immediately after Charming rescued her, she decided she'd never allow herself to be a victim again—and she's got the right hook to prove it. She teaches a self-defense course at the community center called the "Bad Apples," where judo, karate, kickboxing, and bow-staff fighting are all covered. She brings out the best in Charming, especially when it comes to the Grimms. Much to his chagrin, she convinced Charming to apologize to them for decades of rude behavior. This was the first time Charming had apologized in 200 years, and she loved him all the more for it.

FEARSOME FOLKTALES

IN ONE VERSION OF "SNOW WHITE," THE WICKED STEPMOTHER, AS PUNISHMENT FOR TRYING TO KILL SNOW, IS PLACED IN RED-HOT SHOES AND FORCED TO DANCE UNTIL SHE DROPS DEAD.

Awesome!

WHEN THE DOORBELL RINGS,
DO YOU THINK SOMEONE IS COMING
TO KILL YOU?

EVEN YOUR OWN MOTHER?!

ARE YOU AFRAID SOMEONE HAS POISONED YOUR FOOD?

DO YOU FAINT EASILY?

FIND YOURSELF UNABLE TO GET OUT OF BED?

DO YOU FEEL EVEN SEVEN MEN AREN'T ENOUGH
TO PROTECT YOU?

DON'T BE A DAMSEL IN DISTRESS ANY LONGER!

GET EMPOWERED!

LEARN THE FIGHTING TECHNIQUES OF MS. S. WHITE, CERTIFIED MASTER IN:

KUNG FU! / KARATE! / KICKBOXING! / FENCING! / ARCHERY!
HORSEBACK RIDING! / POISON DETECTION! / BALLROOM DANCING!
AND SLEEPING SOUNDLY THROUGH THE NIGHT
(AND THEN SOME)!

SHE CAN TEACH YOU TO USE ANYTHING AS A WEAPON: A BROOM, A MOP,
EVEN A FEATHER DUSTER!

STOP LIVING IN FEAR AND HOPING SOME PRINCE WILL RESCUE YOU. BECOME ONE OF MS. WHITE'S BAD APPLES.
FRIDAY AND SATURDAY AFTERNOONS FROM 4:00-5:00 P.M. AT THE FERRYPORT LANDING COMMUNITY CENTER.

Dee-Dum's WONDERMART

Our Prices Are Insane!

THIS WEEK"S 2 FOR 1 SPECIALS

❄ **DOUBLE TROUBLE GUM**—BUY 1 FOR THE PRICE OF 2!

GEMINI TOILET PAPER—TWO-PLY DOUBLE ROLLS! SHEETS SO THICK THEY'RE IMPOSSIBLE TO FLUSH!

SIAMESE GREEN TEA CAT LITTER—THROW A TEA PARTY IN YOUR CAT BOX!

TWO-WEEK-OLD OYSTERS—SMELL THE ADVENTURE!

TWIN-ENGINE HAT PROPELLERS—PUT SPINNING BLADES ON YOUR HEAD!

COME ON DOWN TO OLD KING COLE'S

FAMILY RESTAURANT

Come on down to Old King Cole's where pipe smoking is still allowed!*

(*restricted to parking lot)

Every Friday Night—Live Music by at least two members of Ferryport Landing's famous hip-hop fiddlers:

The Fiddlers Three!

And Remember, If Old King Cole Isn't Merry, Your Side Salads Are Free!*

(*dressing not included)

Each Kid's Meal Comes in an Edible Bowl!*

(*edible taste not guaranteed)

I give the dumpster 3 stars!

71

SHERIFF ERNEST HAMSTEAD

AKA ONE OF THE THREE LITTLE PIGS

A pink, chubby man with a turned-up nose, Hamstead looks a lot like a pig, which makes sense because he is one. He's the Little Pig who built his house out of straw, and he's the Sheriff of Ferryport Landing. He's unflinchingly brave, always tries to do the right thing, and even defeated the Big Bad Wolf when no one else could. After losing his job to Sheriff Nottingham, Hamstead accompanied the Grimms to New York City where he met Bess, the high-flying Cow That Jumped Over the Moon. It was love at first moo, and Hamstead decided to stay in the big city with his bovine babe. Before saying farewell, he pulled the girls aside and gave them a key to the weapon that would defeat the Wolf if Canis ever lost control.

Girls have cooties—beware!

ANDREW LANG
(1844–1912)

Andrew Lang was a Scottish scholar and intellectual who wrote over 120 books; yet what he's most famous for are the ones he didn't write himself. Like the Brothers Grimm and Charles Perrault, Lang collected and published folk tales. However, rather than writing down stories people told him, he gathered his tales from fairy-tale books written in foreign languages, including those by the Grimms and Perrault. He published twelve beautifully illustrated "Fairy Books" containing hundreds of tales. At that time there was only one fairy-tale book published in English. The common belief was that fairy tales were primitive, brutal, and led to worthless fantasy and escapism—essentially bad for children and too childish for adults. But Lang loved fairy tales and argued that imagination was vital to learning. It helped that he was a serious and respected scholar of mythology and folklore. He published and packaged fairy tales so successfully that English-speaking schoolchildren were finally introduced to these marvelous stories.

Mr. Happyface!

PAINTED BY W. B. RICHMOND, A. R. A.   PHOTOGRAPHED BY F. HOLLYER.   ENGRAVED BY T. JOHNSON.

MR. SEVEN

The seventh of the Seven Dwarfs, Mr. Seven has the most thankless job in Ferryport Landing—he is Mayor Charming's assistant. Charming constantly berates and insults his diminutive manservant, but Charming's attitude toward him changes when Charming gets a glimpse of what Seven becomes in the future—a general in the army fighting the Scarlet Hand. Whether that future will ever come to pass, no one could ever call Mr. Seven "dopey," including the town's resident enchantress Morgan le Fay, who seems to have developed a crush on the little man. Seven has very little contact with his six brothers, who work in the New York City subway system.

FEARSOME FOLKTALES

SNOW WHITE WAS ACTUALLY AWAKENED WHEN THE PRINCE'S SERVANTS, WHO WERE CARRYING HER GLASS COFFIN TRIPPED, DISLODGING THE PIECE OF POISON APPLE IN HER THROAT. SORRY, NO KISS.

THE SHERWOOD GROUP

HAVE YOU BEEN IN AN ACCIDENT OR THE VICTIM OF NEGLIGENCE?

WAS THE ACCIDENT SOMETHING THAT NO ONE WOULD BELIEVE?

ARE YOU AFRAID TO TELL THE POLICE ABOUT YOUR EXPERIENCE BECAUSE IT DEFIES ALL LOGIC? THEN TURN TO THE SHERWOOD GROUP FOR OUR EXPERT LEGAL COUNSEL. WE'LL GET YOU THE MONEY YOU NEED TO GET ON WITH YOUR LIFE—EVEN IF WHAT HAPPENED MAKES NO SENSE!

AT THE SHERWOOD GROUP, WE'RE MERRY MEN, DOING SERIOUS BUSINESS. TURN TO US WHEN YOUR INJURY SEEMS LIKE SOMETHING FROM A BEDTIME STORY. SERIOUSLY.

I blew his head off with my farts

WASHINGTON IRVING
(1783–1859)

Washington Irving was a famous American writer and historian who is best remembered for his two short stories: "The Legend of Sleepy Hollow" and "Rip Van Winkle." Both stories were part of his book *The Sketch Book of Geoffrey Crayon, Gent*, published in 1819. It led to international fame and made him one of the first American writers to achieve respect in Europe. Irving wrote numerous scholarly histories and biographies, but as a young man he started the satirical magazine *Salmagundi* in which, under various pen names, he mocked New York society and politics. Both "The Legend of Sleepy Hollow" and "Rip Van Winkle" take place in upstate New York, not too far from Ferryport Landing.

GOLDILOCKS

One of only five Everafters to find a way out of the barrier, Goldilocks is now a grown woman obsessed with everything being "just right." She's known to come into a house and immediately begin rearranging the furniture—she's an expert in Feng Shui. Unfortunately, she's being pursued by the Black Knight (an agent of the Scarlet Hand) and thus is never in one place more than a few days. Even fifteen years later, Goldilocks still mourns the demise of her love with Henry, whom she considers her true love. It's those feelings that might hold the key to breaking Henry and Veronica's sleeping spell.

True story:
The bears ate her face!

BRIAR ROSE

AKA SLEEPING BEAUTY

With skin like cocoa, bright green eyes, and a soft, ever-present smile, one can understand why Jake was attracted to Briar Rose. But it's her kind, noble heart that caused him to fall in love. Briar now owns a quaint little coffee shop named Sacred Grounds. Jake visits often, but Mallobarb and Buzzflower—Briar's overprotective fairy godmothers—work there, too. They don't know what to make of Jake, finding him an unsuitable suitor for their sweet Briar—he's rough, impulsive, and not even royalty—but those are the things that Briar loves about him.

FEARSOME FOLKTALES

IN PERRAULT'S "SLEEPING BEAUTY," THE PRINCE DOESN'T ANNOUNCE HIS BRIDE TO HIS PARENTS UNTIL AFTER THEY'VE HAD TWO CHILDREN BECAUSE HIS MOTHER IS AN OGRESS THAT EATS CHILDREN. SHE TRIES TO EAT BRIAR AND HER KIDS BUT IS FOOLED.

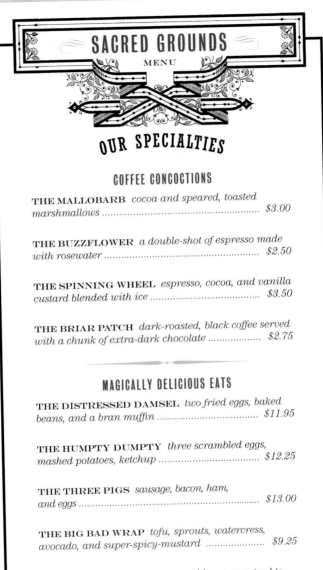

SACRED GROUNDS

MENU

OUR SPECIALTIES

COFFEE CONCOCTIONS

THE MALLOBARB *cocoa and speared, toasted marshmallows* $3.00

THE BUZZFLOWER *a double-shot of espresso made with rosewater* $2.50

THE SPINNING WHEEL *espresso, cocoa, and vanilla custard blended with ice* $3.50

THE BRIAR PATCH *dark-roasted, black coffee served with a chunk of extra-dark chocolate* $2.75

MAGICALLY DELICIOUS EATS

THE DISTRESSED DAMSEL *two fried eggs, baked beans, and a bran muffin* $11.95

THE HUMPTY DUMPTY *three scrambled eggs, mashed potatoes, ketchup* $12.25

THE THREE PIGS *sausage, bacon, ham, and eggs* $13.00

THE BIG BAD WRAP *tofu, sprouts, watercress, avocado, and super-spicy-mustard* $9.25

JUST RIGHT PORRIDGE *porridge guaranteed to be just the way you like it!* $7.25

SACRED GROUNDS

MENU

DESSERTS

FROM THE GINGERBREAD HOUSE

THE ICE QUEEN HEADACHE—*homemade vanilla ice-cream served over a warm marble-brownie* *$7.50*

THE BERRY GODMOTHER—*organic fresh berries, organic yogurt, and granola* *$7.50*

TIME FOR TEA

THE ENCHANTED SLEEP *our home-grown chamomile tea and warm milk* *$2.95*

THE POISONED APPLE *hot and spicy apple-cinnamon tea* *$2.25*

HANSEL AND GREEN TEA *peppermint-spiced green tea* *$2.25*

BRIAR'S ROSE *our home-grown rose-hip tea from organic roses* *$2.25*

CHARLES PERRAULT
(1628–1703)

Charles Perrault was a French writer best remembered for his *Stories or Tales from Olden Days: Tales of My Mother Goose*, a small collection of eight tales, including those about Cinderella, Bluebeard, Little Red Riding Hood, Sleeping Beauty, and Puss in Boots. In seventeenth century France, different classes of society had very little social contact; Perrault rewrote the tales of the common folk so that the wealthier, educated classes would appreciate them. In doing so, he helped turn fairy tales into a literary genre. He was not the first to publish fairy tales, nor did he come up with that term. (Madame D'Aulnoy, a contemporary of Perrault's, is credited with first using it in print.) However, his book marked the first authenticated use of "Mother Goose," which was a type of motherly, country woman. The English used a similar name, "Old Mother Hubbard." (That name goes back to at least the 1500s.) Like the Brothers Grimm who followed, Perrault didn't create these stories. No one knows the true authors, as these tales were passed down orally over generations and changed dramatically along the way.

This kitty just saw Sabrina's face and is now screaming in terror.

UT-3.376 (2011) / FORM 219 • Department of Motor Vehicles

TT# 3 4 2 5 6 2

STATE OF SISTERS GRIMM
TRAFFIC TICKET

For Court Use

SISTERS GRIMM VERSUS

FIRST NAME

RIP

MIDDLE NAME

LAST NAME

VAN WINKLE

LICENSE PLATE NO

ZZZZZZ

CITING OFFICER:

Deputy Boarman

YOU ARE SUMMONED TO APPEAR BEFORE A TRIAL OFFICER

INFRACTIONS:

driving while asleep; reckless driving; expired license; expired
insurance; property damage

NOTES:

Mr. Van Winkle was found asleep behind the wheel of his taxicab, which
had crashed into the Police Station, coming to a halt several feet from
my desk. (This caused Deputy Crane to faint and then wet himself).
Deputy Swineheart arrived moments later to inform me that he'd been
chasing Van Winkle's runaway cab. In addition to the damage to the
station house, the taxi had driven through several front lawns, Old
MacDonald's farm, and the mayor's mansion (destroying several lawn
gnomes).

OFFICER RECOMMENDATIONS:

In addition to fines for speeding and reckless driving, the court
should order restitution for property damage and the dry
cleaning of Deputy Crane's pants.

ZZZ...learning makes me sleepy

ANONYMOUS FEMALE STORYTELLERS

Long before men decided to write down and publish these stories as "fairy tales," they were passed down through generations by anonymous mothers and grandmothers telling the tales to their children by the fireside. Thus, folklore is often known as *old wives' tales*. This is probably why Charles Perrault chose to say his stories were by "Mother Goose," which was a common name for a type of peasant woman. The English had a similar matronly figure, "Old Mother Hubbard," and soon adopted the named "Mother Goose." And even after men like Perrault, Lang, and the Grimms wrote down the stories, it was usually mothers who read them aloud.

MALLOBARB AND BUZZFLOWER

B riar Rose's two fairy godmothers (who are also sisters) never let her out of their sight. They even work with her at her coffee shop. They are incredibly protective and not impressed by Jake Grimm, her boyfriend—they once turned him into a dung beetle. Nevertheless, Jake started to win their affection with his dedication to Briar and his bravery. The two fight furiously against the forces of the Scarlet Hand.

 FEARSOME FOLKTALES

IN THE STORY "DONKEY SKIN," A PRINCESS RUNS AWAY BECAUSE AFTER HER MOTHER DIES, HER GRIEF-STRICKEN FATHER DECIDES TO MARRY HER.

THE COUNCIL OF MIRRORS

The Hall of Wonders holds many secrets—the biggest is that it's actually a backdoor into twenty-five other magic mirrors created by the Wicked Queen. Unfortunately, most have been destroyed or are far too dangerous to enter, but the five remaining mirrors become invaluable assets in the family's fight to stop the Master.

The first mirror is home to a 1970's nightclub called the Disco of Wonder, complete with glittering ball and multi-colored dance floor. Its guardian, Donovan, wears an astrology medallion and likes to shake his booty.

The second mirror is the home of the Diner of Wonders—a soda fountain from the 1950's featuring a roller-skating waitress named Fanny.

FEARSOME FOLKTALES

IN THE GRIMMS' "HANSEL AND GRETEL," THE CHILDREN WERE ACTUALLY SENT INTO THE WOODS TO GET LOST AND DIE.

Great parenting!

The third mirror hosts a happy go-lucky fellow named Reggie with a thick Jamaican accent and dreadlocks. Inside his reflection is the Warehouse of Wonders, filled with crates formerly owned by the murderous Bluebeard.

In the fourth mirror resides the uproarious Titan—a burly Viking with a love of fighting. His mirror reveals a dark and disturbing dungeon known as the Hall of Doom.

The fifth mirror is shrouded in mystery. Some say it's Alice's mirror, which transports one to Wonderland. Others say it's inhabited by a devilish guardian who cannot be trusted. No one really knows for sure.

PART FOUR

ENEMIES

JACK THE GIANT KILLER

AKA JACK ENGLISHMAN

In his glory days, Jack was the king of killing giants, reportedly ending the lives of ten of the Big Ones during his storied career. But times change. Fast forward a few hundred years, and Jack found himself in trouble with the law and working as a suit salesman at Harold's House of Big and Tall. When Sabrina and Daphne met him, he was broke and desperate to reclaim his glory. It didn't work out according to plan, as dozens of furious giants came down from the sky to administer giant justice. Before the Giant Queen took him back to her Cloud Kingdom, Jack threatened the Grimms one last time, shouting, "The Scarlet Hand is coming, and your days are numbered!"

Loser

"I've got bigger plans than selling shoes and measuring hemlines. These beans are going to make me a hero again. but for that to happen ... the Grimms have to die."

I killed 3 giants this morning.

Magic beans = Magic farts!

THE MAGIC BEANS

These little white beans may seem harmless, but carelessness with them can rain chaos on the world. Once planted, they sprout a massive beanstalk that grows miles into the sky, opening a door into a kingdom built on clouds. They are one of only a few magical items that are capable of breaching the barrier surrounding Ferryport Landing but are impractical as an escape route because the trip is only one-way. Jack used the beans to release a giant he then tried to kill. What few beans remained were kept in a mason jar in the Hall of Wonders until Jack stole them in an effort to escape the town and regain his fame as a giant killer. In his battle with the Grimms, he dropped the remaining beans on the ground and was soon surrounded by giants who carried him away.

MAJOR MOMENTS IN SCARLET HAND EVIL

The goal of the members of the Scarlet Hand is to free themselves from Ferryport Landing, and united with Everafters from around the globe, enslave humans and rule the world. After several failed efforts to secure their freedom, many of the members have concluded that the only real way to destroy the barrier is to kill the Grimm family.

- Oz kidnaps Henry and Veronica Grimm, leaving a red handprint on the dash of their abandoned car.

- Jack the Giant Killer has a red handprint on his chest, revealing that he serves the Hand. Working closely with the Master, he tries to kill the Grimms to put an end to the barrier.

- Rumplestiltskin reveals the Scarlet Hand is a movement, not a person, and it will rule the world.

- Rumplestiltskin feeds on the raw emotions of children then transforms it into an explosive energy he hopes will destroy the barrier and allow the Scarlet Hand to take over the world.

- The Master puts Little Red Riding Hood and the Jabberwocky in charge of watching over Henry and Veronica. Red has covered them with red handprints.

- The Queen of Hearts and Sherriff Nottingham take over the town, harassing the Grimms and all of their friends.

- Time tears send the girls fifteen years into a future where the Scarlet Hand rules the world.

- A mob, fueled by the Scarlet Hand, arrests Canis for murder then tries, convicts, and sentences him to death.

- The Scarlet Hand sends the Black Knight after Goldilocks to prevent her from waking Henry Grimm with a kiss.

- The Master steals Veronica and Henry's unborn child in hopes of giving birth to his dark vision of the future.

- Pinocchio infiltrates and betrays the Grimms as a member of the Hand.

"Oh, I have many names,
but the one I like best is
Daddy."

CASPER SHEEPSHANK

AKA RUMPLESTILTSKIN

When Sabrina first met her school guidance counselor, Mr. Sheep-shank, she was taken in by his warm, understanding personality. He seemed to realize how hard it was to be a kid and assured Sabrina that she was always welcome to vent her frustrations to him. Little did Sabrina know that her recently worsening headaches, paranoia, fistfights, and outbursts of rage were caused by her new "friend." Sheepshank revealed his true hideous form—that of Rumplestiltskin—a three-foot-tall monster covered in kinky-brown hair who was feeding on the raw and uncontrolled emotions of children he would then turn into his slaves.

> **FEARSOME FOLKTALES**
>
> RUMPLESTILTSKIN'S NAME MEANS "LITTLE RATTLE STILT." A "RATTLE STILT" IS A KIND OF DEMON.

Since when is turning kids into **zombies** a bad thing?

ARE YOU MAD?

ARE YOU A PUNCHING BAG FOR THE LOCAL BULLY? ARE YOU DROWNING IN HOMEWORK? DOES YOUR TEACHER MAKE YOU WANT TO PULL OUT YOUR OWN HAIR?

SCHOOL SURE CAN BE A BUMMER! IN FACT, IT CAN MAKE A PERSON DOWNRIGHT ANGRY. **BOTTLING UP THOSE FEELINGS ISN'T GOOD FOR YOU.** RECENT SCIENCE PROVES THAT HOLDING IN YOUR ANGER CAN CAUSE YOU TO BURST INTO FLAME, EXPLODE, AND THEN POSSIBLY EVEN DIE! WHO NEEDS THAT? YOU NEED SOMETHING OR SOMEONE IN WHICH TO CHANNEL ALL THOSE POWERFUL FEELINGS.

LET THAT PERSON BE ME!
JOIN MR. SHEEPSHANK'S RAGE STARS!

RAGE STARS IS THE ONLY AFTER SCHOOL PROGRAM THAT HELPS YOU LEARN ABOUT YOUR FEELINGS AND DIRECT YOUR ANGER TOWARD MORE PRODUCTIVE PURSUITS. PLUS, IT'S FUN! YOU'LL LEARN:

- PRIMAL SCREAM THERAPY
- ANGER MANAGEMENT
- ASSERTIVENESS TRAINING
- PADDED-CLUB-BASED THERAPY
- EMBRACING YOUR HOSTILITY

EVERYONE UNDER THE AGE OF 12 IS WELCOME!
THE CLUB MEETS MONDAY THRU FRIDAY IN THE BASEMENT BOILER ROOM. BRING A SHOVEL!

You should see what Dorothy's gym socks could do!

DOROTHY'S SLIPPERS

Formerly owned by the Wicked Witch of the East, the slippers then came into the possession of young Dorothy Gale when her house falls on the wicked sorceress. They're actually more silver than red, though they have a rosy glow in the light and adjust to fit the wearer. To use the slippers, the wearer clicks her heels and repeats where she wants to go three times in a row. In a flash, the person is transported. However, they do not have the ability to take the owner out of the barrier. Sabrina uses them to take herself, Daphne, and Jack to Charming's ball. Daphne realized they could use the shoes to find their parents—but one of the slippers was lost, making the other useless.

THE WIZARD OF OZ

AKA OSCAR ZOROASTER PHADRIG ISAAC NORMAN HENKLE EMMANNUEL AMBROISE DIGGS

The great and terrible Oz is not really a sorcerer, but what he can do with machines is nothing short of magical. At his job at Macy's department store, the Wizard of Oz created realistic mechanical illusions for Christmas window displays. When meeting the girls he revealed a whole side to their mother they never knew—Veronica was a highly respected advisor to a secret community of Everafters living in New York City! Oz claimed to be one of her best friends, but he betrayed her to the Master, kidnapping Veronica and Henry and turning them over to the Scarlet Hand. When confronted, he quoted the Master who said Sabrina's parents would "Give birth to a future where Everafters ruled the world."

Couldn't you give
Sabrina a brain
too?

L. FRANK BAUM

(1856–1919)

L. Frank Baum was a former window dresser who wrote fifty-five novels, four-teen of which centered on the life and times of the citizens of Oz. *The Wonderful Wizard of Oz* was published in 1900 and is often referred to as an American fairy tale. Though Baum created the story himself (as opposed to having it told to him), Baum admitted a desire to emulate the stories of the Grimms and Hans Christian Andersen. However, he wanted to invent new creatures rather than just use the typical fairy-tale characters. He also wanted to get rid of the strict moral lessons of the typical Grimm stories. The Oz books were a tremendous success. When Baum passed away in 1919, his publisher turned the series over to Ruth Plumly Thompson, who added another twenty-one books to the collection. The Oz stories have been adapted into feature films, stage plays, musicals, and dozens of official sequel books, as well as a variety of reimagined novels and comics.

THE QUEEN OF HEARTS

The Queen of Hearts is quite a sight—bloodred lips, purple eye shadow, mahogany eyebrows, and a black hole of a beauty mark on her left cheek. Sadly, there's not a lot of inner beauty, either. As mayor, she uses her power to make the Grimm family miserable. Ultimately, she wants nothing more than to rule Ferryport Landing as insanely as she ruled Wonderland, and if anyone gets in her way, they may just lose their heads.

--- magical object! ---
THE FROG WAND

Amongst Baba Yaga's many magical items was a wand capable of transforming a person into a frog. In an effort to steal another powerful weapon, Sabrina snuck into Baba Yaga's frightening house. When confronted by the witch, Sabrina turned the wand on her. Unfortunately, the spell backfired, and suddenly Sabrina found herself acquiring a taste for flies.

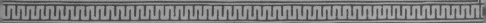

LEWIS CARROLL

AKA CHARLES LUTWIDGE DODGSON
(1832–1898)

Lewis Carroll created some of the craziest characters in literature in his novels *Alice's Adventures in Wonderland*, and *Through the Looking Glass, and What Alice Found There*. He used nonsense and word play to tell weird and wild stories. Carroll made up the story of Alice while on an outing with some young friends, a girl named Alice Lidell and her two sisters. Carroll might have just forgotten the story had Alice not insisted he write it down. Eventually, he published it and became a worldwide success. He followed it up with the sequel, *Through the Looking Glass, and What Alice Found There*. The monstrous Jabberwocky comes from a nonsense poem in that book. Carroll's inventiveness was not limited to storytelling. He came up with a number of clever gadgets, and invented word games and puzzles, including an early form of Scrabble. He was also an accomplished mathematician and a master of the early art of photography.

THE "DRINK ME" BOTTLE & "EAT ME" CAKES

These tasty treats first appeared in Lewis Carroll's, *Alice's Adventures in Wonderland*. "Drink Me" makes a person small, while the "Eat Me" cakes make you big. Once sold at Tweedledee and Tweedledum's convenience store, they are now kept in the Pantry, a room in the Hall of Wonders for perishable goods.

SHERIFF NOTTINGHAM

The famous villain from the Robin Hood tales, Sheriff Nottingham, has a scar that runs from the corner of his mouth to his eye. It grows purple and pulsates when he's angry, which is most of the time. He carries a dagger everywhere he goes and threatens to slash anyone who gets in his way. Before he was elected (replacing Hamstead), he promised he'd commit every waking hour to putting the Grimms behind bars. He made a powerful enemy in Jacob Grimm, and the two seem destined for a deadly confrontation.

magical object!
SATIN SURGEON'S SALVE

Originally written about in *A Thousand and One Nights*, this healing wonder comes in a tin that reads, "Now with a lemony fresh scent!" However, it's an icky black ointment that smells like backed up sewage. Jake used it to heal Sabrina's broken arm, and Ferryport Landing's resident Nurse Sprat saved Jake's life with it after Nottingham shot him with a crossbow. Sprat also put it on Little John's hand when, in frustration while training on the fairy wands in the Hall of Wonders, he punched a column and broke his hand. What little remains is in the possession of Nurse Sprat.

"Don't cry, little one. Save your tears. You'll need them sooner than you think."

"The Master ... wants to keep the mommy and daddy and baby brother. He wants me to paint the red hands everywhere I go."

LITTLE RED RIDING HOOD

The story of Little Red Riding Hood can send shivers down anybody's spine, but the actual events are even scarier. Whether her troubles began before her encounter with the Wolf or after he killed her grandmother is debatable, but somewhere Little Red lost all touch with reality. Proven to be mentally unstable and dangerous, she was placed in a hospital the day she arrived in Ferryport Landing. After several escapes, Spaulding Grimm and Baba Yaga cast the same spell on the asylum that was cast on the town decades before. There Red stayed until Jake Grimm turned off the barrier, inadvertently freeing the little girl and the monstrous Jabberwocky she came to regard as a pet. Soon, she became a pawn of the Master, who used her to look after Henry and Veronica. After her madness was cured, she came to live with the Grimms.

Best story ever!

FEARSOME FOLKTALES

IN AN EIGHTEENTH CENTURY FRENCH VERSION OF "LITTLE RED RIDING HOOD," RED IS FOOLED BY THE WOLF INTO EATING HER GRANDMOTHER'S COOKED FLESH AND DRINKING HER BLOOD.

FERRYPORT LANDING

ASYLUM

PATIENT MEDICAL RECORD

PATIENT NAME
Little Red Riding Hood

PATIENT CASE NUMBER:
#67

DIAGNOSIS:
psychosis
with delusions
and hallucinations;
homicidal tendencies

ATTENDING NURSE:
SPRAT

NOTES:

One hundred fifty years of treatment and still crazy. What's new to report? NOTHING. She's still obsessively drawing and painting her "family"—a father, a mother holding a baby, a grandmother, herself, a kitten, and a ferocious looking dog (guess who that is?). No medications have helped. She's still prone to horrific screaming, creepy singing, and biting—many fitful nights of sleep. Most of the staff has swept her under the rug and it seems some days that I'm the only one who will even bother with her now. I feel for the child—she is really quite innocent in all this, but it's becoming more than I can stand. Some of the nurses suggested that Red killed her grandmother herself and blamed it on the Wolf. I can't believe that. I think there is something good in her somewhere.

JABBERWOCKY

The Jabberwocky is a creature of few words, and all of them are "Jabberwocky." But you don't need to say much when you're fifteen feet tall with scaly skin, black leathery wings, a massive serpentine tail, monstrous feet, hands as big as a man, and a mouth filled with thousands of jagged fangs. When Wilhelm set sail for America on the *Neuer Anfang*, he brought ten Jabberwockies.

---

magical object!

THE VORPAL BLADE

In Lewis Carroll's book, *Through The Looking Glass, and What Alice Found There*, Alice reads the poem "Jabberwocky" about a knight who kills a monster with a magical sword called the Vorpal blade. In 1909, Spaulding Grimm had the Blue Fairy break the blade into three pieces because it was too powerful and could be used to cut through the barrier. He hid the pieces but had inscribed clues on them in case they ever needed to be reassembled.

But they escaped en route and were all killed below decks by the Black Knight using the magical Vorpal blade—the only weapon that can kill a Jabberwocky. Yet somehow, a Jabberwocky survived and appeared in Ferryport Landing in 1909. Along with Little Red Riding Hood, it created a path of destruction throughout the town while the family scrambled to find the missing pieces of the Vorpal blade.

THE LITTLE MATCH GIRL'S MATCHES

These mysterious matches were made famous in Hans Christian Andersen's tragic tale of "The Little Match Girl." The user simply strikes a match and makes a wish. Whatever the user desires will be seen within its flickering flames. Charming had the last two matches in existence and gave them to the Grimm girls explaining they could be useful in finding their missing parents. This incredible act of generosity by Charming made Sabrina feel profoundly guilty for judging all Everafters as wicked.

Stay Out of My Stuff!

Male seeking Female for long walks on the beach, romantic dinners, and counting my treasures. Must have a hunger for life and respectful of other people's private things.

YOU CAN CALL ME: Bluebeard

SIGN: Pisces

LAST RELATIONSHIP: It's complicated.

ABOUT ME:

My heart is as blue as my beard. I'm a multi-time widower with a room full of sad memories, but it's time to open the door to my heart and find my soul mate. I'm a rugged 6'5" and haven't aged a day since turning thirty-five. (You'll never guess my real age ladies!). I'm from the old country but have set firm roots in Ferryport Landing. I guess I'm an optimist, because I know there's always an easy solution to my problems. I love to laugh, and even when enraged, I can quickly find humor in most events. Even funerals don't get me down for long! Tomorrow's always a new day and a chance to meet that new mate! Could it be you?

— magical object! —
MERLIN'S WAND

This wand once belonged to King Arthur's powerful wizard, Merlin, but somehow ended up at a garage sale in Athens, Ohio. Jake bought it from an old man who thought it was a back-scratcher. To use, one must flick the wand and ask for what one wants. Before realizing her dangerous addiction to magic, Sabrina used it to summon lightning bolts. When Baba Yaga demanded the wand in exchange for her portion of the Vorpal blade, Sabrina tried to steal it back, only to fail and be turned into a frog.

THE BLACK KNIGHT

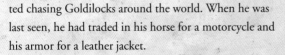

The Black Knight has a sordid and storied past that goes all the way back to the time of King Arthur, but whether he is friend or foe is dependent on the day of the week. As he sailed for the New World with the rest of the Everafters, Wilhelm turned to him when a pack of Jabberwockies ran wild on the ship, and he heroically saved the day. When another Jabberwocky terrorized the town, the Black Knight's fighting skills were required once more. Instead of killing the beast, he used a magic sword to escape the Ferryport Landing barrier. Nothing had been heard of him in hundreds of years until he was spotted chasing Goldilocks around the world. When he was last seen, he had traded in his horse for a motorcycle and his armor for a leather jacket.

---

magical object!
EXCALIBUR

The legend of King Arthur's fabled sword has been told for hundreds of years. Some say it's a sword created by fairies. Others claim it was a gift from the water elemental, the Lady of the Lake, and still others claim it was buried inside a stone until the true king pulled it free. Amongst its rumored magic is the ability to protect the user from any harm, but Sabrina is told its true enchantment is its deadly edge. Even the tiniest nick from its steel can cause a person to drop dead. Sabrina used it to kill a rampaging giant.

CARLO COLLODI

AKA CARLO LORENZINI
(1826–1890)

Carlo Collodi was the pen name for Italian writer Carlo Lorenzini, who is most famous for writing *The Adventures of Pinocchio*. Parts of the story were published weekly in the first Italian newspaper for children. Sadly, Collodi died before his famous story went on to worldwide acclaim, but his timeless tale has been the inspiration for countless books and feature films—including Disney's animated classic.

PINOCCHIO

O nce upon a time, Pinocchio wished he was a real boy, and like magic, this marionette became living, breathing flesh. Unfortunately, he should have been more specific with the Blue Fairy because he hasn't aged a day since and is stuck in a little boy's body. After hundreds of years away from his father, Gepetto, he came to Ferryport Landing for a remedy. He turned to the Master, who promised to alter the spell if he would spy on the Grimms. Despite the Grimms' kindness, Pinocchio betrays them using his own magical marionettes to steal the keys to the Hall of Wonders and release what is locked behind its doors. Sadly, when it came time to win his reward, Pinocchio discovered that this former puppet was played by his master.

PRINCE ATTICUS

Prince Atticus is the mysterious brother of Prince Charming—so mysterious that Charming had no idea that he existed. He appears to be a mirror image of William. Unlike the dashing and heroic former mayor, Atticus is diabolical and murderous—and seemingly bent on killing his brother. Very little is known about Atticus—only that he was once married to Snow White and because of his terrible nature was imprisoned in a magical book called *The Book of Everafter.* There the Wicked Queen, Snow's mother, tried to erase him but could only force him into a state of non-being in the book's margins. Now he's back with revenge on his mind and a bloodstained mace in his hand.

Ooooh, I'm SO scared—
Not!

Ferryport Landing would be impossible without the magical substance that makes its human residents forget some of the crazy things that happen in the town. A little pinch induces amnesia, which comes in handy after a giant attack or a street fight between witches. Granny always keeps an ample supply in her handbag, and the former mayor, William Charming, ordered a ton of it dumped on the town every night. Who knows, maybe you've come into contact with forgetful dust—not that you'd remember.

Ruin it for everyone, SPOILER!

THE MASTER

For years, the identity of the mysterious Master haunted the Grimm family. After all, he was responsible for the kidnapping of Henry and Veronica, as well as a score of frightening and violent incidents. Though the girls had their suspicions, no one could have imagined the villain would be living in their own home. It was Mirror who revealed himself and his two faces—both figuratively and literally. In his desperate attempt to free himself from the Hall of Wonder, he kidnapped Henry and Veronica's newborn baby and tried to take over his body. Luckily, Granny Relda foiled the plan but had to sacrifice herself. Now this wicked creature has complete control of her mind and body. Granny Relda will do anything to protect her family and uphold the family motto: "We are Grimms and this is what we do."

"That red handprint... It's quite a unique symbol—intimidating, powerful. Don't you agree, Relda?"

126

AFTERWORD

Phew, it's over! I thought it would never end. It just went on and on.
I was sure we'd all have long white beards by the time the author
decided to wrap this thing up. Well, luckily, after a little persuasion
and a beehive stuffed in his underwear drawer, the author realized
it was time to step aside and give the fans what they really want—
my Ultimate Guide!

From here on out the rest of this book will knock your socks off.
You're going to love it because it's not stoooooopid like the first 126
pages. Nope, from now on you're going to be in awe of my villainous
history—like the time I set fire to a village of tiny blue people, or
how I used to swipe human babies and replace them with goblins,
or even my years as a television executive. It's evil stuff!

Wait! What do you mean this is the end of the book? The "end"
end? But there are only two lousy pages about me. Oh, this is
ridiculous. I demand more pages. What am I going to do about it?
Do you see this sword? Sure it's small and made of wood but—
hey! Don't disrespect the sword! Take that! Yeah, it hurt! It was
supposed to. Now, I'm thinking maybe I deserve my own book. We
can call it "Everything You Ever Wanted to Know About Puck But
Were Too Dumbstruck by his Awesome to Ask." What do you mean
bookstores will complain about that title? That title rules! Are you
arguing with me? You want more of the sword, buster? I didn't
think so.

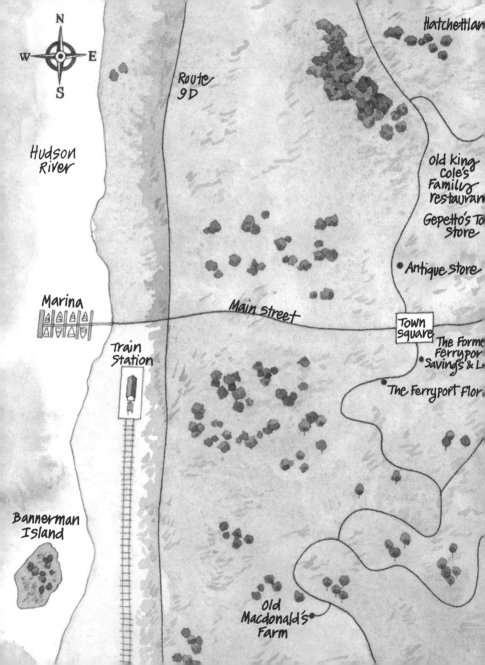